Gwen

Tough Luck

Editorial Director: Marge Kennedy
Retold by John W. Kennedy
Based on Ben 10 Episode #22 by Steven T. Seagle

little monks on the wisdom tree

Hex is back!

He is joined by his nefarious niece, Charmcaster.

PROLOGUE:
Prison Break

The siren blared as the guards scrambled into action. An unauthorized intruder had entered the maximum-security penitentiary.

As they raced to the point of the security breach, the guards were amazed to see an ashen-haired teenage girl wearing a long purple coat. She carried a handbag with a strange design on it that looked like the head of a sea creature.

"Hold it!" shouted out the lead guard.

But the girl did not answer. Instead, she responded by hurtling a purple ball of energy that exploded in the middle of the prison ward, disabling the alarm and sending a dozen guards tumbling backward into the titanium walls!

As the other sentries drew their weapons, the girl opened her bag and threw still more energy orbs, creating havoc as she effectively subdued them all!

Then, with the dozens of guards overpowered

and unconscious, the petite trespasser confidently walked past several cells.

She knew exactly where she was going as she proceeded down the long corridor leading to the top-security cell at the very center of the facility.

As she approached, the lone guard at the end of the hall swung shut a 24-inch-thick super-security door in a last-ditch effort to prevent the teen interloper from reaching her intended destination.

With eerie calmness, she reached into her strange purse and removed still more energy orbs. She threw them at the door. The guard on the other side could only watch in growing fear as the orbs dented the supposedly impenetrable passage.

BOOM! BOOM! BOOM!

The pounding sound of the energy spheres echoed louder and louder through the chamber where the brave but frightened guard prepared to make his final stand.

Then…*BANG!*

The door flew off its hyper-diamond hinges!

The guard raised his gun to fire, but the

sheer force of the final energy orb blast sent him somersaulting backward into the wall!

He was knocked out cold as the mysterious teen girl walked toward the center chamber's single cell. This was the super-reinforced holding pen, reserved for the facility's most notorious and dangerous criminal.

Charmcaster again reached into her bag. As she removed her hand from the inside of her purse, she spread a sparkling purple powder that adhered to the outside of the final prison door. Then she spoke the mystical words, "***Ballun Qarkata Minagaam!***"

A purple energy field began to surround the perimeter of the cell's door, which was even thicker than the one she had just blasted through.

The hum of accelerating energy permeated the area until the door was suddenly blasted into smithereens!

The girl peered inside.

There, standing at the other end of the dark space, was the eerie silhouette of a hooded man whose back was turned toward her.

"Charmcaster," the mysterious figure said, "I've been waiting for you."

"Major jailbreaks aren't exactly easy to pull off, you know!" she complained.

"You will show me respect, my dear niece," the shadowy prisoner responded, "or you will suffer the consequences."

"Yes, Uncle Hex," Charmcaster replied as he turned toward her, revealing a skeletal face and eyes that seemed to glow in the dark.

"My staff!" he demanded.

Charmcaster reached into her purse and pulled out a long walking stick that was carved into the shape of snake with a vulture's head. It should not have been able to fit in the bag.

"The magic must have drained out of it," she explained nervously. "It doesn't work. It's not my fault," she pleaded as her uncle seemed to will the cane toward himself.

"Its powers can only be brought to life in the hands of a master magician," Hex declared.

Then, suddenly, the prison alarm began blaring once again as a second wave of guards ran to the scene!

Hex raised his staff. Powerful bolts of energy shot forth. The oncoming officers were knocked unconscious before they even knew what hit them!

"Now to find the Keystone," the sorcerer single-mindedly proclaimed. "The moment of alignment is nearly upon us."

Hex then pointed his staff toward his cell's supposedly indestructible solid stone wall and effortlessly blasted a huge hole through it as Charmcaster looked on in awe.

When the smoke cleared, a magic carpet lay beneath them.

Hex and his niece then looked out into the dark night and the secluded woods. Hex vowed, "Once I have completed the ritual and gained the powers of the Keystone, I shall take my revenge on the one responsible for imprisoning me in this festering sewer."

With that, the carpet lifted off the floor. Hex and Charmcaster soared away into the darkness.

Left behind on his prison wall were a taped-up newspaper article and photo of Lucky Girl (Secret Identity: 10-year-old Gwen Tennyson). That masked young superhero, against all odds, had defeated the mighty sorcerer in a cataclysmic battle of good versus evil.

Now, young Gwen Tennyson's faith, courage, and strength were about to be tested again. Would she be ready?

CHAPTER ONE:
The Keystone of Bezel

The tour bus, filled with senior citizens, teetered on the brink of Red Rock Canyon after losing its brakes along Highway 14 en route to Las Vegas.

"No one move!" warned the driver, who worried that a single misstep could send the vehicle toppling over the side of the road.

But sitting still was not an option either, as the bus started tilting further toward the abyss. The passengers screamed as the vehicle was about to plunge into the canyon!

Then, just as it was about to fall, something grabbed the bus from behind.

The passengers breathed a huge sigh of relief until they looked through the rear window and saw that the bus was being saved by a giant, multi-limbed monster!

As they began screaming once again, the creature ripped off the rear of the bus and roared,

"It's okay, everybody! Everything's all right now! You're safe!"

The passengers breathed another sigh of relief when they realized the monster they initially feared was actually out to help them. Though they did not know his name, that "monster" was actually Four Arms, the alien superhero from the planet Khoros.

Or, still more precisely, Four Arms was Ben 10, Gwen Tennyson's 10-year-old cousin, whose DNA was connected to a watch-like device called the Omnitrix.

Ben had found the Omnitrix – or it had found him – while exploring the woods during a camping trip earlier that summer. Since then, he had been able to transform into superheroes from throughout the universe.

Whenever there was danger, Ben could be counted on to press the special button on the Omnitrix, become an alien hero, and save the day!

As Four Arms helped the elderly passengers and the bus driver to safety through the back of the bus, Gwen watched from the rear window of the Rustbucket, their Grandpa Max's beat-up Recreational Vehicle (RV).

Though she was happy to see the people rescued, she wished that she was the superhero doing the rescuing.

"Oh, Lucky Girl," she sighed while twiddling her black and purple superhero mask in her hand, "if only you were more than just another Halloween costume."

But, once upon a time she was.

Gwen first became Lucky Girl when she, Ben, and Grandpa Max visited New Orleans. That's where they had their first encounter with the evil sorcerer Hex, who was on a quest to gather the Charms of Bezel, an ancient set of jewels that individually possessed powers over fire, levitation, reincarnation, and luck.

Together, however, the charms were far more powerful. Whoever had them all could harness the powers of the universe!

Hex had acquired them all except the jewel empowered with luck. Through a quirk of fate, that gem had fallen into Gwen's possession. She had used its power to set in motion seemingly impossible lucky occurrences. She donned a mask, and the news media soon began calling her Lucky Girl.

But, in the end, Gwen realized that the Charms

of Bezel were too dangerous to risk keeping. So, after defeating Hex and taking the gems, she chose to destroy them all, releasing their power back into the universe.

By doing so, she gave up the superpowers the magic jewel had bestowed upon her, and she returned to being just plain Gwen Tennyson, an ordinary girl who was overshadowed by her superhero cousin.

But Gwen's remembrance of what she gave up was interrupted when Ben slammed open the Rustbucket's door and hopped inside.

"This hero stuff is getting old fast!" he complained.

"You should be proud of yourself," Grandpa Max said. "Those folks would've been in a real pickle without you."

"I know," he said, "but I'd like just one regular summer day where I can just hang out and do nothing. You know, like Gwen," he said, gesturing toward his cousin.

"You should appreciate what you have," Gwen advised while lamenting, "I only got to be Lucky Girl for a day."

"Really?" Ben grinned, "Because, with all the bragging you did, it felt like weeks."

Gwen threw a pillow at her annoying cousin. Ben ducked just in time.

"That's enough," Grandpa Max said, smiling. "We still have to talk about where to go next on our road trip."

"Maybe we could follow the bus," Ben joked. "The old folks were on their way to some lame-o magic convention in Las Vegas. How corny can you get?"

"Magic convention?" Gwen repeated with interest.

"Oh, no!" Ben sighed. "Why'd I open my big fat mouth?!"

Meanwhile, several miles away, Hex and Charmcaster stood before a bonfire in the woods.

"*Takara Doratyn Agosto!*" Hex called out as the image of the Keystone of Bezel materialized above the flames.

"Magic amulet, reveal your location to me!" the warlock demanded. Then, before their eyes, the Keystone's image was replaced by some kind of eerie holographic map.

"What's it say?" Charmcaster asked.

"Yours is not to ask questions," Hex replied imperiously. "Yours is to follow."

"Yes, Uncle, of course," Charmcaster meekly responded.

The next day, the Tennysons arrived at the Magic Lamp Hotel in central Las Vegas, where the Magician of the Year Convention had already gotten underway.

As they entered the large convention hall, Gwen examined the various kiosks. There were assorted card tricks, linking rings, shiny scarves, and other magic paraphernalia. The weird wares were being hawked by amateur illusionists, who all looked like this was their first foray out of the house in quite some time.

"It's all cheap junk and gross-out tricks!" Gwen griped. "I thought this was going to be about magic magic, not cheesy magic."

Ben, on the other hand, was pleasantly surprised as he reached into a bin of cheap toys.

"Check it out!" he laughed. "Fake bugs in ice cubes! Fake barf! Fake dog poo!"

"Ben, we get it," Grandpa Max groaned with sympathy as he patted his disappointed granddaughter on the head.

"As long as we're here," he continued, "we might as well look around."

The Tennyson trio separated and began exploring the aisles.

Gwen approached a corner booth that was getting little attention from the other convention goers.

Beneath an overhead sign reading "Magic Jewels," a large exotic-looking woman sat inside the kiosk behind a table that was filled with a collection of odd trinkets and fake jewelry.

"I don't suppose you have any real magic artifacts," Gwen asked.

"What you see is what you get, honey," the woman replied in a distinct Brooklyn accent.

Nonetheless, Gwen perused the various knickknacks and ornaments for no other reason than to pass the time.

While rummaging through a collection of bracelets and charms, she came across a strange bracelet that reminded her of the Keystone of Bezel, a gem she had only read about online. It was said to combine and multiply tenfold the powers and abilities of anyone who possessed it.

"Could it be?" Gwen wondered as she reached into her purse.

"I'll take it!" she said as she impulsively paid the one-dollar asking price.

"Did you find something you like?" Grandpa Max asked, startling her from behind as Ben stood next to him.

"Yeah," Gwen replied. "It kinda reminds me of..."

But before she could complete her sentence, a wave of screams filled the hall. The sound was coming from outside the hotel.

The Tennysons ran toward the sidewalk, where spectators were looking up in horror as an out-of-control helicopter dangled a straightjacketed upside-down escape artist on the end of a 20-foot cord!

"SOMEBODY HELP ME!!!" screamed the terrified performer as a helpless crowd watched from below.

"I don't think that's part of the act!" Grandpa Max exclaimed.

"I know, I know," Ben said as he prepared to press down on his Omnitrix. "It's hero time!"

CHAPTER TWO:
The Return of Lucky Girl

With a helicopter careening wildly above the Vegas Strip and a helpless escape artist dangling from a tether, Ben knew that he had to act quickly.

Activating the Omnitrix on his wrist, he became...STINKFLY!

Wasting no time, the giant insectoid alien flew upward as the chopper spun around and whipped the panicked escape artist through a grouping of power cables, igniting a spark that threatened to burn through his lifeline!

Gwen and Granpda Max, now separated by other onlookers, watched the drama unfold, hoping that Ben, as Stinkfly, could save the swaying acrobat. Stinkfly soon latched onto the skids at the bottom of the copter!

"Everything's under control!" he called out. He used every ounce of his strength to try to steady its wobbly flight path before it tumbled into the crowd below.

But then one of whirlybird's blades suddenly came loose and spun toward Grandpa Max!

"Grandpa! Look out!" Gwen shouted as she somersaulted over two cars and pushed him out of the blade's deadly path just in the nick of time!

"How'd you do that?" Grandpa Max asked with amazement.

"Just lucky, I guess," she replied as her just-purchased bracelet began to glow.

Meanwhile, up above, Stinkfly was barfing out a web of alien goop that attached itself like a web to the surrounding hotels. The material held the wayward helicopter in its grasp, steadying it.

"Just hold on!" Stinkfly yelled down to the dangling escape artist.

But, at that very moment, the ember that was burning through his tether caused it to snap. The crowd gasped as the performer plunged toward the street!

Fortunately, Gwen, now wearing her Lucky Girl

costume, raced to the scene. She quickly bounded over a parked car and bus to grab the falling showman in midair! Together they fell onto a hotel canopy, which broke their fall!

"Lucky Girl?" said a shocked Stinkfly as he landed on the scene amid the cheers of the surrounding crowd.

"Don't even start with me about 'cramping' your superhero style," Gwen warned as she basked in the glow of her heroic rescue. Clearly, she was enjoying the attention.

"Hey," Stinkfly responded, "I'm just happy to finally get a little back-up. How'd you get your Lucky Girl powers back?"

"I'll tell you later," Gwen responded as she took one more bow for her gathered fans.

Later, back in the Rustbucket, Gwen was at her laptop studying a picture of the Keystone of Bezel as Ben looked on.

"That looks just like the thing on your bracelet," Ben observed.

"It's one of the Charms of Bezel," she said.

"But you destroyed them during that fight in the cemetery with that Hex creep," Ben recalled.

"Not all of them," Gwen replied. "This is the legendary Lost Keystone. It's rumored to multiply by ten the powers and abilities of anyone who possesses it."

"You are sooo lucky!" Ben said with envy.

"It's not luck," Gwen insisted. "It's magic."

A short while later, the Tennysons were back at the convention center where the Magician of the Year contest was taking place.

"And remember," the emcee hyped, "the Magician of the Year will be named in less than an hour during the height of today's solar eclipse! Now, please welcome our next contestant, The Amazing Allan!"

In a plume of white smoke, The Amazing Allan appeared on stage. He was wearing a puffy white shirt and had waist-length blond hair. Next, he pointed to a mysterious box on wheels.

"For my first trick," said the foreign-born illusionist, "I'll need a volunteer from zee audience."
Ben sensed an opportunity for some fun.

"Ben Tennyson at your service!" shouted the impish 10-year-old, already on stage and startling the trickster.

"What's he up to?" Grandpa Max moaned with dread.

"Pleez get into zee Magic Cube," The Amazing Allan requested as he opened the top of the box.

"Whatever you say," Ben said as he climbed inside.

"Ein boy goes in," the showman announced in his heavily accented English, "but what comes out vill amaze and zurprize you!"

"Yeah, they won't be the only ones," Ben snickered to himself while inside the box.

The Amazing Allan then locked the top of the box and spun the cube around several times, demonstrating that there were no secret hatches from which Ben could escape.

In grandiose fashion, the magician waved his arms about as he said, "*Abracadabra!*"

But as he reached forward to unlock the box, it suddenly began to shake violently.

Ben, as Four Arms, comes to the rescue!

Gwen makes a magical find!

Lucky Girl returns!

Now there are two superpowered Tennysons!

Ben volunteers for mischief.

Wildmutt's out of the box!

Evil descends upon the city!

The Tennysons consider their next move against Hex and Charmcaster.

Realizing this was not part of his planned routine, The Amazing Allan made himself disappear by running off the stage in a panic!

Then the Magic Cube, which could not hold its contents, exploded. Wildmutt, the huge alien canine from Ben's Omnitrix, burst forth onto the stage to exuberant audience applause!

Witnessing the enthusiastic crowd response from offstage and sensing victory in the Magician of the Year contest, Allan returned to the stage and nervously took his bow. He hoped that the large, fanged creature next to him wasn't hungry.

Then a swirl of crimson-red smoke descended through the skylight and onto the already crowded stage.

POOF! Standing before the crowd were Hex and Charmcaster!

Gwen and Grandpa Max watched with great concern as The Amazing Allan jealously confronted the show crashers.

"Hey, wait your turn!" he demanded.

"You're ruining my amazing magic act!"

"I have no time for amateurs," Hex thundered. With a wave of his arms, he levitated the faux wizard a few feet off the ground, sending him colliding into Wildmutt and knocking them both off the platform!

He then looked directly at Gwen and demanded, "Give me the Keystone of Bezel!"

CHAPTER THREE:
Super Family Feud

"If it's magic you want, it's magic you shall have!" Hex declared as he sent forth waves of fiery energy into the terrified assembly.

The show goers stampeded toward the exits in fear. This was far more magic than they had bargained for! Then, with a wave of his sorcerer's staff, Hex slammed the doors shut, trapping everyone inside! The people begged to be let go, but Hex ignored them.

Grandpa Max turned to Gwen and said, "Hex is up to his old tricks!"

Gwen darted behind a column, proclaiming, "This looks like a job for...

"Lucky Girl!" she finished as she emerged on the other side of the pillar clad as the costumed superhero!

"Hand over the Keystone or I shall destroy you all!" Hex commanded.

"You forgot to say, 'pretty please,'" Lucky Girl taunted as she leaped onto the stage for her rematch with the evil wizard.

"The Keystone and Lucky Girl! How convenient!" Hex sneered as the convention center doors suddenly swung open, allowing the frightened audience members to flee.

Hex raised his staff and prepared to cast a spell on Lucky Girl.

"Morbius..."

But before he could complete his incantation, Wildmutt jumped on top of him, knocking the warlock to the floor and wrapping his mighty jaws around his staff!

Hex wrestled Wildmutt for control of his magic stick, but he was no match for the astoundingly strong alien beast!

"Charmcaster!" Hex called out in desperation. "Do something!"

"Yes, Uncle," she obeyed. Reaching into her bag of tricks, she hurled powerful magic discs at Wildmutt, forcing the space canine to release his hold on Hex's supernatural walking stick!

Hex crawled out from beneath the wolverine creature. He then used his staff to fire a stream of high-voltage electric bolts at the ferocious hero, throwing him backward into an abandoned kiosk!

Meanwhile, Lucky Girl was charging Charmcaster, who wielded yet another magic disc. She maliciously tossed it toward the approaching superhero, knocking her off the stage.

Sensing imminent victory, Charmcaster looked down on the groggy heroine. She smiled as she prepared to finish her off! But, just as she was about to throw another magic disc at the fallen Lucky Girl, her concentration was broken by a flying bowling pin, which struck her in the shoulder.

As Charmcaster turned around, she saw Grandpa Max on the other end of the room – armed with more bowling pins! She tossed the magic disc she had intended for Lucky Girl at him! The disc grew in size as it flew across the arena. Grandpa Max jumped out of the way as it rolled past him and exploded against the wall!

Grandpa Max's action gave Lucky Girl the opportunity she needed to recover. She got up and took a judo leap at Charmcaster, kicking her to the floor.

Then, it was time to once again face Hex.

"There are two kinds of luck, child," said the malevolent master of magic. "Let me show you the bad kind!"

"Guess what?" Gwen answered.

"Now that I've got the powers of the Keystone, I'm not just lucky anymore! I am TOTALLY KICKBUTT!" She then grabbed the shocked spellbinder's staff and flipped him over her shoulder.

Getting up, Hex proclaimed, "Even with your new superpowers, you are no match for a master magician! Now, GIVE ME THE KEYSTONE!"

Just as Hex was about to cast another spell, Wildmutt hurled a stage amplifier at him, forcing him to dive for cover.

Hex was furious – and a bit dazed.

Lucky Girl was about to charge toward the temporarily disoriented villain when she was blocked by Charmcaster, who threw two small stones into her path.

"Is that the best you got?" Gwen taunted.

But, before her eyes, the rocks began transforming into huge creatures of black magic that resembled nothing she had ever seen before!

"Then again," she wryly amended her previous statement, "that's pretty good."

The two hideous beasts approached Lucky Girl, forcing her to back into a corner! Just as they were about to pounce, Wildmutt leaped into the battle! Together, they fought the two monsters from the netherworld until the behemoths exploded into nothingness!

Surprised, Lucky Girl looked toward Charmcaster and saw that she had just been knocked over by a piece of stage furniture that Grandpa Max had slid across the floor. Once Charmcaster's concentration, which had given life to the vile beasts, was broken, so were they!

As Charmcaster stood up, Wildmutt jumped on top of her!

"Get off me!" she shouted as she emitted an upward wave of energy that sent Wildmutt flying into the air! She then blasted a hole in the floor so when Wildmutt came down, he fell all the way down to the hotel's basement.

All this action gave Hex the time he needed to revive. Now he was angrier than ever!

"ENOUGH!" he commanded. He unleashed a powerful force that pushed Lucky Girl and Grandpa Max through an exit that led to a spectacular outdoor garden.

When they finally came to a stop, the two Tennysons found themselves in the middle of a man-made maze of hedges.

"Where's Ben?" Grandpa Max asked with concern as they attempted to get their bearings.

But there was no time to talk, as the stones around them began rolling forward and transforming into several of the same monsters Lucky Girl and Wildmutt had fought earlier!

Lucky Girl and Grandpa Max ran away from the oncoming stampede of beasts, but the monsters were gaining fast! It seemed that this time Lucky Girl's luck had run out!

As the Tennysons continued to run through the confusing maze, they accidentally split up. The creatures continued to chase them both.

Grandpa Max soon found himself running down a dead end with one of the beasts hot on his trail! He turned around and watched as the monster charged him. There was no escape!

Then, just as the beast leapt at him, Wildmutt jumped over the bush and immediately engaged the monster in fierce combat!

Then...POOF! Like the others, it blew up and disappeared.

A second later, Wildmutt transformed back into Ben.

"That was close!" Ben panted.

"Apparently," Grandpa Max reasoned, "if these things lose their connection to Charmcaster, they cease to exist."

"Yeah," Ben agreed, "but where's Lucky Girl?"

At that moment, Lucky Girl was on the other end of the maze, standing over Charmcaster and holding her bag of tricks.

"You're not so tough now, are you?" Lucky Girl said triumphantly.

"I-I didn't mean to hurt anybody," Charmcaster stammered. "My uncle made me do it!"

"Why should I believe you?" Lucky Girl asked with skepticism.

"I'm sorry about all of this," Charmcaster said meekly. "I have to do what my Uncle Hex tells me to do. He doesn't take 'no' for an answer.

"I can help you!" Charmcaster added. "He's after the Keystone in your bracelet."

"Well, duh!" Lucky Girl mocked. "I know that! He wants to magnify his powers!"

"But that's not all!" Charmcaster warned. "If he performs the Ritual of Bezel with the Keystone at the highest point during the eclipse, he can re-create all the powers of all the other charms you destroyed!"

"That would be terrible!" Gwen said.

"ARE YOU MAKING NEW FRIENDS, CHARMCASTER?!" The hedges shook as a spectral Hex walked through them and appeared before the startled girls.

As he materialized before them, he raised his

hand toward the sky, where Ben and Grandpa Max floated helplessly above!

"Give me the Keystone," he demanded, "or watch your loved ones suffer a painful demise!"

"Don't listen to him, Lucky Girl!" Grandpa Max shouted.

"Grandpa Max is right!" Ben added, while struggling in the sorcerer's invisible grip. "You can't let Hex win!"

As Hex's hold on them grew tighter and tighter, Gwen was tempted to give in to his evil demand.

"I won't let you do this, Uncle!" Charmcaster cried in defiance.

She grabbed her bag of tricks from Lucky Girl. Opening it, she unleashed a thousand flying bats that flew directly toward Hex.

"Charmcaster!" the angry wizard bellowed as the winged rodents carried him off into the distance. "How dare you betray me?!"

Charmcaster then gently lowered Ben and Grandpa Max to the ground.

"I guess you are legit," Lucky Girl said as she offered her hand in friendship to Charmcaster.

"Thanks," Charmcaster said, reciprocating. "But," she fretted, "my uncle's gonna be really, really mad at me."

"Don't worry," Lucky Girl reassured her. "You stay with Grandpa Max. Ben and I will deal with your uncle."

"Thank you," Charmcaster said. She hugged Lucky Girl, while choking back tears. "I'll never forget how you freed me from his control."

"It's okay," Lucky Girl responded softly.

Then, she and Ben ran off in the direction of Hex.

The magic showdown was at hand!

CHAPTER FOUR:
Misdirection

Lucky Girl and Ben followed the bats as they carried Hex away and dropped him into the hotel fountain.

As the Tennyson heroes arrived on the scene, the sinister sorcerer emerged from the pool, standing atop a water spout and looking more powerful than ever!

Ben pressed down on his Omnitrix – but nothing happened!

"The power of the watch is still drained from our last fight," Ben reported. "I need time for it to recharge!"

"That's okay," Gwen responded, "Lucky Girl can handle this!"

Lucky Girl then leaped toward her arch adversary – but fell flat on her face!

"What's wrong?!" Ben asked with a sense of urgency.

"My powers are gone!" Gwen responded.

"That can't be good," Ben matter-of-factly replied as the wicked warlock neared.

"GIVE ME THE KEYSTONE!" Hex thundered as he levitated the helpless heroes toward himself. He then grabbed Lucky Girl's wrist and looked at her bracelet.

"Hmm," he smirked to himself as he released the Tennyson cousins from the grasp of his power and allowed them to tumble onto the hotel lawn.

"We'll meet again," he promised as he disappeared in a burst of flame.

"Uh, what just happened?" Ben asked as he scratched his head.

Lucky Girl looked at her bracelet. "The Keystone! It's gone!" she exclaimed.

"How?" Ben questioned.

"Misdirection," she answered, while remembering Charmcaster's hug of gratitude back at the hedge maze.

"What?" Ben replied.

"It's what magicians do to fool their audiences," Gwen explained.

"So, you mean," Ben realized, "that lame-o hug she gave you before was just a distraction while she lifted the Keystone from your bracelet?"

"Exactly," Gwen replied. "I guess I'm one dumb former superhero."

Meanwhile, Hex and Charmcaster had reunited on the roof of the nearby Zenith Hotel.

"Pretending to betray me was genius," Hex congratulated his deceitful niece, "but you should have informed me of your plan first."

"Yes, Uncle," Charmcaster agreed, "but I had to think fast."

"No matter," Hex smugly replied while clutching the Keystone. "Soon I shall have enough power to destroy all my enemies and rule the world!"

A short time later, Ben and Gwen, still dressed as Lucky Girl, found Grandpa Max lying unconscious outside the Rustbucket in the hotel parking lot.

"Grandpa Max, what happened?!" Gwen asked as he came to.

"I turned around for just a second – and wham!" Grandpa Max answered. "When I came to, Charmcaster was gone!"

"All that 'my uncle made me do it stuff' was an act," Gwen informed him. "She needed to get close enough to me to steal the Keystone. Some superhero I turned out to be."

Feeling defeated, Gwen removed her Lucky Girl mask.

"Gwen," Ben interjected, "even superheroes make mistakes. Right now our job is to stop Hex and Charmcaster."

"If Hex performs the Ritual of Bezel at the highest point during the eclipse, he can re-create the powers of all the other charms I destroyed," Gwen said.

"That's less than a few minutes away," Ben noted as the moon drew closer to blocking out the sun.

"But how do we find them in time?" Gwen worried.

"What's the 'highest point' around here?" Grandpa Max asked.

"The radio tower above the Zenith Hotel!" Gwen exclaimed.

"Then, let's go!" Grandpa Max replied as they raced toward the scene.

Meanwhile, on the Zenith rooftop, Charmcaster

watched as Hex levitated the Keystone of Bezel toward the top of the tower in convergence with the start of the solar eclipse.

"*BALUBAN HESTIDA XERXAM!*" he repeated over and over as the sky darkened.

Streams of powerful energy began emanating from the floating Keystone. At that moment, Hex and Charmcaster saw Lucky Girl hovering in midair beside the building.

"Did you really think you could ditch me that easily?!" Lucky Girl called out.

"What is going on here?! How are you flying?!" the baffled Hex questioned.

"The powers of the Keystone – and all the Charms of Bezel – are flowing into me, not you!" Lucky Girl replied.

"No, this can't be!" the rattled wizard fretted.

"But it is!" Lucky Girl shot back. "Now surrender the Keystone, or I'll be forced to take it from you! You dare not face the awesome powers of Lucky Girl!"

"This is totally bogus!" Charmcaster contended to her confused uncle. "She can't have any superpowers. It's some kind of stupid trick!"

"Don't you think I know that?!" shouted the agitated spellbinder. He then levitated the superhero upward. As she rose, Grandpa Max, who had been crouched on a window-washer's platform, rose too. Their attempt at illusion had failed.

Hex then dropped them both atop the roof, knocking the wind out of them as they landed.

"Your silly stunt has gained you nothing!" he gloated as he looked down on them from his pedestal. "Now prepare to die at the hands of the all-powerful Hex!"

Gwen and Grandpa Max looked up helplessly as the sinister sorcerer wielded his glowing staff and prepared to administer his death spell!

"*WAHOO!*" Ben shouted as he zoomed onto the scene aboard a hoverboard, a surfboard-like device once given to him by a space alien ally. He rode the board into Hex, throwing him from his mighty perch.

Stunned, Hex was now helpless as he plummeted toward the street below.

As Ben aimed his hoverboard downward to rescue their falling foe, Gwen looked up at the shaken

Charmcaster and, with a smile, chided, "You should know better than anyone that sometimes magic is about misdirection."

But this fight wasn't over yet!

CHAPTER FIVE:
Power Play

As the Keystone of Bezel continued to hover above the Zenith Tower, Ben caught the falling sorcerer Hex aboard his hoverboard!

But, far from feeling gratitude toward the young superhero for saving his miserable life, the rescued wizard began fighting him for control of the flying craft!

Meanwhile, on the hotel rooftop, Charmcaster reached into her bag and tossed magic stones into the path of Lucky Girl and Grandpa Max. As the pebbles exploded, a pink mist whisked them backward into an idle roller coaster ride atop the hotel across the street.

Charmcaster then took out another magic stone and lobbed it at the coaster, setting it in motion. She cast three more stones at the track up ahead, causing the rails to disappear.

Looking ahead at the ominous gap, Gwen screamed, "We're not gonna make it!"

Before Grandpa Max could respond, the Tennysons' roller coaster car began falling through the breach. A horrified crowd watched from the street below.

At the same moment up above, Hex swung his staff at Ben, causing him to lose his balance and fall off the hoverboard!

As he fell to earth, Ben pressed his Omnitrix, but nothing happened!

"Come on!" he shouted at the watch as he pressed it again. But, again, nothing!

Hex then directed the hoverboard back toward the Zenith rooftop just as the eclipse was at its climax.

"I'll take it from here, Charmcaster," he directed his niece as he deboarded the craft.

"That would be a big 'NO,' Uncle," she responded with surprising defiance.

"What?!" Hex replied with shock.

"There's been a change in plans," said Charmcaster. "I get the power of the Keystone and the Charms of Bezel – and you get squat!"

"You dare defy me!" the sorcerer raged as he sent a beam of fiery energy at his rebellious niece!

With the Keystone still hovering above the tower, Charmcaster responded by shooting forth powerful magic energy of her own, which, to Hex's dismay, grew more powerful as his weakened! He soon found himself falling helplessly into the hotel's air-conditioning system!

"Charmcaster, why?" Hex pleaded as he sank into the metal contraption.

"It's simple," his nefarious niece answered coldly. "I just needed a master magician to perform the re-creation ritual. While you were fighting the kid, I took the opportunity to absorb the Powers of Bezel for myself!"

"Not so fast, Charmcaster!" Lucky Girl called out from the other end of the roof.

Charmcaster turned around and was shocked to see the masked heroine flanked by Grandpa Max and the large leafy alien known as Wildvine, from Ben's Omnitrix.

The trio glared at the wayward witch.

"I-I don't understand," Charmcaster stuttered. "I saw you crash in the roller coaster!"

"Maybe," Lucky Girl suggested, "if you weren't

so intent on stealing the Powers of Bezel you'd have noticed that Wildvine showed up just in time to grab my grandpa and me before the coaster hit the ground."

"Good thing the third time was the charm with the Omnitrix," Wildvine whispered to Grandpa Max.

"Now why don't you just give up," Lucky Girl said as she picked up Hex's staff.

"That staff only works in the hands of a master magician," Charmcaster scoffed.

Lucky Girl aimed a powerful energy ray from Hex's magical rod. To her surprise, Charmcaster let out a cry and fell, defeated, to the ground. The magic gems then rose into the air and formed a circle above Wildvine. He took them into his hands and crushed them. A powerful explosion followed as Charmcaster's evil power flowed out of her and disappeared into the air.

"Do you know what you've done?!" Hex shouted, still stuck in the air-conditioning machinery.

"Saved the day?" Ben asked.

At that moment, the Keystone landed at Gwen's feet. Reluctantly, she picked it up.

"It looks like the magic's gone," she said sadly. "And Lucky Girl is gone, too," she added.

"Don't be too bummed," Ben said, trying to console her. "There are lots of other ways you can be a hero."

Gwen eyed his hoverboard.

"Like riding on a hoverboard?" she asked.

"It takes a lot of practice to figure out how to drive these things," Ben said, getting an awful feeling that the competition between him and Gwen for super status wasn't over yet.

Gwen hopped on the flying craft.

"Then I'd better get started! *Wooo!*" she shouted as she took off, expertly steering it in circles around Ben.

Two superheroes prepare for battle.

Dangerous surfing!

Whoa!

Showdown!